It was a rare, bright October day in South Florida — clear skies with not a storm in sight, despite it being hurricane season. Priscilla recalled a time when hurricane parties filled the boardwalk in Hollywood, Florida. Down here, no one seemed to care much about hurricanes.

But her focus wasn't on the weather; it was on getting her bookstore ready for its grand opening. **Where are these contractors?**" she thought, frustration bubbling up. She had been waiting for days to get the new bookshelves installed. Rushing into the bookstore, she scanned the bare walls and picked up her phone to text Tiffany. Before she could hit the send key, Tiffany walked in.

"Hey girl, what's up?" Tiffany said, her voice was light and carefree.

Priscilla sighed. "I'm so frustrated. I've been trying to get these bookcases put up for months. I want to open this place as soon as possible."

"Stop worrying. They'll be here," Tiffany reassured her, motioning for her to sit down. "Relax."

"I'm trying to, but juggling the salon and this store is driving me crazy," Priscilla admitted, pacing back and forth.

The two friends walked through the adjoining door into the salon. Every chair was filled with customers, the hum of conversation blending with the buzz of hairdryers. Things seemed to be going well.

"Hi, everyone," Priscilla greeted before heading into the back office, Tiffany close behind.

"So, I actually came down here because I wanted to see if you wanted to go to Hard Rock tonight," Tiffany said excitedly. "There's a new club, and it just opened."

Priscilla raised an eyebrow. "Tiff, do you ever work?"

Tiffany scoffed playfully. "Girl, I landed you this prime location with side-by-side businesses with an adjoining door. It made me a lot of money and brought in new clients. So, yes, I do work."

They both laughed. Before Priscilla could respond, her phone rang. The contractors.

"They're finally here!" she said, rushing out to meet them.

A worker stepped forward. "Ms. Mason, I apologize for the delay. Traffic on I-95 was terrible."

Priscilla rolled her eyes. "I believe that. The snowbirds coming down from up north always make it worse this time of year." She gestured toward the empty spaces. "Let me show you where I want everything."

As the contractors unloaded the shelves, Tiffany waved goodbye. "See you tonight!"

Priscilla locked up the bookstore later that evening, sighing in relief. **Finally, some progress.** She called Tim, letting him know she was meeting Tiffany at Hard Rock later and asked if he wanted to join them.

"Yeah, I'll meet you guys there," Tim agreed before hanging up.

At home, Priscilla took a quick shower, lay down, and unintentionally dozed off. A loud ringtone jolted her awake.

"Girl! Where are you?" Tiffany's voice boomed through the phone. "I've been calling you for hours!"

"I must've dozed off," Priscilla muttered, rubbing her eyes. "Getting up now. Did Tim get there yet?"

"I don't see him," Tiffany shouted over the music.

Priscilla sighed and quickly called Tim, leaving him a message before heading out. Arriving at the Hard Rock, she handed her keys to the valet, weaving through the sea of people. Just as she put away her phone, she bumped into someone—a tall, striking man.

"Oh, I'm so sorry! I was rushing to meet a friend," she said.

"No worries. I wasn't watching where I was going either," he said with an easy smile. "After you."

They walked in the same direction, and Tiffany, standing in front of the club, waved. She hugged Priscilla before whispering, "Who's that good-looking man?"

"Not sure. We literally bumped into each other," Priscilla said.

Tiffany wasted no time. "Hi, I'm Tiffany! And you are?"

"James. James Jones."

"Well, Mr. Jones, we were just heading inside. Care to join us?"

"Sure. I'm actually supposed to meet someone, but I don't see them."

As they entered, James kept glancing at Priscilla, though Tiffany was absorbed in talking about herself. A reggae beat dropped, and James turned to Priscilla. "Care to dance?"

The music was infectious, the rhythm pulling them together. As they danced, Priscilla felt a strange pull toward him. She turned around, looking up at him, their eyes locked. **What is this?** she thought, shaking her head. **I have a boyfriend.**

James gently took her hand as the dance ended, leading her back to Tiffany.

"He likes you," Tiffany whispered.

"I have someone," Priscilla reminded her, just as her phone buzzed. A message from Tim.

"Hey, babe. Can't make it tonight. I'll see you tomorrow. Have fun. Tell Tiff I said hi

Priscilla sighed, slipping her phone into her purse. Tiffany gave her a knowing look.

"He's not coming, huh?" Tiffany asked.

Priscilla shook her head.

"Forget about him. Let's go have fun!" Tiffany exclaimed, dragging her onto the dance floor.

James approached them. "I've got to head out. The person I was meeting isn't coming, and I have an early day tomorrow." He handed Priscilla his card. "Call me sometime."

She tucked the card away and waved goodbye as Tiffany pulled her back into the music.

Saturday Morning

Priscilla rolled into the Dunkin' drive-thru for her usual medium caramel macchiato and an old-fashioned doughnut before heading to the salon. As she parked outside, she took a moment to admire how much she had accomplished. **Mom would be so proud.**

A memory surfaced.

"Priscilla."

"Yes, Mom?"

"Come here, please."

She had walked into her mother's room, sitting beside her on the bed.

Her mother had held her hand, her voice barely above a whisper. "You know I don't have long. I just want you to know how proud I am of you. I see the long days and nights you put in. Everything you do for me—I see it all." She coughed. "I love you. Never forget that."

Priscilla had leaned forward, kissing her mother's cheek. "I love you too, Mom."

A week later, the elder Mrs. Mason had passed away at home from cancer.

Sitting in her car now, Priscilla wiped away a tear and took a deep breath before heading inside. Today was a new day.

Priscilla's Weekend

Priscilla wiped the tears from her eyes as the memory of her mother's words faded. With a deep breath, she stepped out of her car, unlocking the salon doors. Today, the contractors wouldn't be in, but a group of teens were coming to help sort books for the store.

She sipped her macchiato while setting up her station for her first client, Mrs. Bailey. Music played softly in the background as the other stylists trickled in, their greetings filling the space. As usual, chatter turned to Instagram gossip and Friday night outings. Priscilla simply listened as she worked, washing, blow-drying, and curling Mrs. Bailey's hair—prepping her for Sunday service.

Once finished, she retreated to her office, shutting the door behind her. **Finally, a moment of quiet.** She reached for her phone and dialed Tim.

"Hey, babe. What's up?" he answered.

"Just here in the office, waiting for the kids to show up for the bookstore," Priscilla said. "What about you?"

"Just hanging out with the brothers, chilling."

She nodded, though he couldn't see it. "Alright, I'll talk to you later. I think I hear them coming now."

Priscilla stepped outside just as the teens arrived, their energy filling the space.

"Hi, Miss Priscilla!" they called out.

She smiled. "Alright, let's head over to the bookstore so I can show you what needs to be done."

Leading them inside, she pointed toward stacks of boxes overflowing with books. She assigned each person a section, designating one teen as the lead before heading back to her office. As she dropped her purse onto the desk, a small card fluttered onto the surface.

James.

Without thinking, she picked it up, dialed the number, and—voicemail. She hung up almost immediately. **Why did I just call him?** she thought, shaking her head.

Returning to the bookstore, she found the teens half-working, half-recording TikTok and selfies.

"You all better be working—I'm not paying for a social media session!" she teased.

"Aww, Miss Priscilla, we were on a break," one of the girls protested.

"This is a lot of work," another chimed in.

"Well, if you want to work here after school, you have to start from the bottom and work your way up."

"We know," they all groaned in unison.

Smiling, she rolled up her sleeves and helped one of them organize the display counter. **One step closer to opening day.**

Sunday Reflections

The sunlight streamed through Priscilla's bedroom window, promising a warm, peaceful day. **Perfect for lounging by the pool.**

She headed downstairs, scrambling eggs, toasting rye bread, and steeping a cup of green tea. As she ate, her thoughts drifted toward Tim. **Is this still the road I want to travel?**

Her mind rewound to the day they met—a chance encounter at Albertsons on University Drive. He had been standing near the deli when she walked up to place her order. A brief exchange, a glance, and they went their separate ways. Days later, fate intervened again, this time at a gas station. He approached her as she reached for the pump.

"Let me get that for you," he had said, taking the nozzle.

That was two years ago. Back then, everything had felt effortless. But after her mother passed, Priscilla's focus had shifted to work—her businesses, her goals. Tim, a contractor, was always on the move, traveling between Miami, the Keys, and even Fort Myers. Time apart had become routine.

Shaking off her thoughts, she placed her dishes in the dishwasher and headed upstairs to shower. A crop top and shorts seemed perfect for the day. Grabbing a book and her sunglasses, she stepped outside, settling into a chair by the pool.

The rhythmic sound of water lapping against the edges, the warmth of the sun—it lulled her into sleep.

A Dream or Reality?

"Hey there, why are you alone on such a beautiful day?"

Priscilla squinted against the sun, only able to make out a tall, dark silhouette. The voice was familiar.

James.

He sat down beside her, casually taking the book from her hands.

How did he get back here? Did I leave the gate open? The thought sent a wave of unease through her.

Without a word, James stood, peeled off his shirt, and dove into the pool.

"Are you coming in?" he called, laughing. "The water's perfect."

She walked over to the edge. "I don't have a swimsuit."

Without hesitation, he grabbed her hand and pulled her in.

Water surrounded her.

Laughter.

Electricity.

"What are you doing here?" she asked, breathlessly. "And how do you know where I live?"

Then—

"Priscilla! Priscilla!"

Tim's voice.

Her eyes snapped open. Tim was standing over her, gently shaking her shoulder.

"I have a key… what are you talking about?" he asked, puzzled.

Heart racing, she looked around. **A dream. Just a dream.**

Tim sat onto the chair beside her, searching her face. "What were you dreaming about?"

"Oh, nothing." She forced a laugh. "Just tired from the bookstore. I wanted to relax and must've dozed off."

"You've been busy," he admitted. "I barely see you anymore."

"What about you?" she countered. "I know work keeps you busy."

"Same old, same old," Tim sighed. "Workers who don't want to work, putting more pressure on me."

He squeezed her hand. "I'm going to head inside and change. You need anything?"

She shook her head, watching him go.

Was I really dreaming about James? The thought unsettled her.

After a few hours of lounging, Tim returned. "Hey, P, want to hit Ginger Bay later? I've got a craving for Escovitch fish and jerk wings."

"That sounds perfect," Priscilla said.

As evening approached, she went inside to get ready. Tim was still in the pool. **That man is going to be a prune when he gets out.** She chuckled.

Then—her phone rang.

A number she didn't recognize.

"Hello?"

"Hi, this is James Jones. I got a call from this number yesterday."

Priscilla's pulse quickened. **Oh, no.**

"Oh—uh—hi, James." She hesitated. "Yes, I called but got your voicemail. I didn't want to disturb you, so I hung up."

"You should've left a message," he said smoothly. "I wouldn't have given you my card if I minded."

She glanced toward the pool—Tim was still there. She hurried upstairs.

"Well, now you have my number. Make sure you save it."

"I definitely will," James said. "Actually, can I ask you something?"

"Sure."

"Can we meet for coffee or tea this week?"

Her breath hitched. She hesitated—then, "I'll call you tomorrow and see when's a good time."

"Looking forward to it," he replied.

As the call ended, a slow realization crept in.

What am I getting myself into?

Without wasting time, she called Tiffany. **She needed advice.**

Final Preparations & A Secret Romance

Weeks passed, and Priscilla had been working tirelessly to complete the bookstore. The teens came after school each day, helping stack and organize books, and now everything was nearly done. If all went as planned, the grand opening would take place the week before Christmas.

Outside of work, her mornings had taken on a new rhythm—coffee with James. They had grown closer, their meetups feeling as natural as breathing. He had memorized her order—a macchiato and an old-fashioned doughnut—ordering it before she even arrived. **It was as if they had been together forever.**

Yet, Priscilla had kept certain details from him. He didn't know the location of her shop. He didn't know about the grand opening. And most of all, he didn't know about Tim. James never pressed for more, so she allowed things to stay as they were.

Tiffany walked into the bookstore, eyes wide with admiration. "Girl, you have done an amazing job. I am so proud! Are you ready for the grand opening?"

Priscilla exhaled, allowing herself a moment of satisfaction. "Yes! Invitations are sent, the caterers are booked. Tomorrow, I will start decorating."

As if on cue, Tim walked in, carrying a Christmas tree. "Hey, Tiff," he greeted, giving her a quick hug. He turned to Priscilla. "You see what your girl has done? Looks great, doesn't it?"

Tiffany grinned. "I love it."

Tim nodded, setting the tree down. "Where do you want it?"

Priscilla pointed toward the window. "Right there."

As Tim assembled the tree, she and Tiffany leaned against the counter, going over the final plans.

Then—her phone rang.

James.

Tiffany glanced at her knowingly. Priscilla hit voicemail.

"You're still seeing him, huh?" Tiffany asked, smirking.

"Every day," Priscilla admitted with a laugh. "Tim is hardly ever around. I've been asking him to bring this tree for weeks! James… he's different. He just gets me."

"You said that about Tim," Tiffany teased, "but I won't lie, James is fine."

They laughed.

"I'm thinking of inviting him over tonight," Priscilla said, lowering her voice.

Tiffany raised an eyebrow. "And Tim?"

"He's probably going to Miami."

Priscilla turned toward Tim. "Babe, I'm hanging out with Tiff tonight. Want to come?"

Tim shook his head. "Nah, I have an early appointment in the Keys."

Priscilla threw Tiffany a look. **See?**

That evening, Priscilla sent James her address, instructing him to have the gate attendant call her upon arrival. In the kitchen, she prepared grilled salmon drizzled with orange liqueur sauce, avocado and mango salsa, and yellow rice. A bottle of wine chilled nearby as she went upstairs to get dressed.

She slipped into a sleeveless black Vera Wang maxi dress, paired with strappy sandals. A spritz of Alfred Sung Forever lingered in the air just as her phone rang.

"Yes, let him in," she instructed the attendant.

Moments later, James stood at her door, the scent of his cologne sending a thrill through her. She exhaled sharply.

Focus, Priscilla.

She hugged him, lingering just a second too long.

"Wow, you smell good," she murmured.

He grinned. "And you look amazing."

Inside, James admired her home. "I knew you had it going on, but this…"

She handed him a glass of wine. "You hungry?"

James smirked. "Brains and beauty, plus she can cook. Impressive."

She laughed. "Come on, let's eat."

After dinner, they moved poolside, the night air cooled against their skin. Wrapped in each other's arms on the chaise lounge, their lips finally met.

Morning After & New Dilemmas

The next morning, Priscilla woke to a text from Tiffany— **'Give me all the details.**

Shaking her head, she slipped out of bed, grabbing her phone. **This girl.**

At Dunkin', James already had her coffee and doughnut waiting. This time, when they parted ways, she gave him a soft, lingering kiss.

Later, she finally called Tiffany.

"I *knew* you two were going to get closer! I saw it in your eyes!" Tiffany said excitedly.

"Hush, Tiff," Priscilla blushed.

Tiffany's tone shifted. "This is getting messy, girl. Are you going to break up with Tim or keep both?"

Priscilla sighed. "I don't know."

"Did you tell James about the grand opening?" Tiffany asked.

"No. Tim is going to be there, so I don't think I should."

Tiffany sounded skeptical. "And you think James is cool with that?"

"He doesn't pressure me," Priscilla said quickly. "Plus, he has something to do that night."

Tiffany hesitated. "Okay… but be careful."

"I will," Priscilla assured me before hanging up.

Grand Opening Approaches

The bookstore shimmered with holiday cheer—twinkling lights, garland, and a towering Christmas tree. The scent of cinnamon and pine filled the air.

"Miss Priscilla, where do you want these flowers?" a teen helper asked.

"Set them by the register," she said.

With everything in place, she locked up for the evening and headed home. **Tomorrow, the doors will officially open.**

Excitement buzzed within her—but so did uncertainty.

Would her tangled relationships remain a secret?

The Grand Opening

The Christmas lights twinkled brightly, casting a warm glow through the bookstore's windows. Outside, a crowd gathered, their chatter blending with the festive music playing softly inside. The tree stood tall, adorned with ornaments that sparkled like tiny stars. Priscilla moved through the room, greeting guests as they wandered among the shelves. Her family had come, their words of pride filling her heart. **Mom would've loved this.**

Tiffany darted around, ensuring the caterers had everything they needed. The teens, dressed sharply, helped wherever they could, their youthful energy adding to the celebratory atmosphere.

Priscilla tapped her glass, the sound ringing out like a bell. The room quieted, all eyes turning toward her.

"Good evening, everyone," she began, her voice steady but filled with emotion. *"I'd like to welcome you to Asmara's Journey. Here, you'll find books from all over the world. I've searched high and low to ensure there's something for everyone. This day has been a long time coming a dream I've held close to for years."*

She paused, her gaze sweeping the room. *"As a child, I remember reading The Taming of the Shrew by William Shakespeare and wondering how many others had read it, why I found it so fascinating. I told myself, one day, I'll sell this book so everyone can read it. That love for reading grew—I devoured three books a month, dreaming of teaching English. But my true passion was sharing the gift of reading. And so, this is my gift: opening Asmara's Journey."*

Her voice softened. *"Asmara means 'beautiful butterfly.' Like butterflies, we grow through stages to become something extraordinary. This bookstore reflects that journey—from infancy to adulthood, nurturing minds with knowledge. Thank you all for being here tonight. Enjoy."*

Applause erupted, filling the room with warmth. Guests approached her, shaking hands, offering congratulations, and snapping photos. Priscilla's heart swelled with joy.

A Shocking Encounter

Tim appeared, a bouquet of flowers in hand. "Hey, babe. I loved your speech. Glad I made it just in time."

Priscilla smiled, kissing his cheek. "Thank you."

As she turned to greet another guest, Tim wandered off to mingle. The night wore on, the crowd thinning but still lively. Tim approached her again, his expression eagerly.

"I want you to meet someone," he said.

"Give me a few minutes," Priscilla replied, heading toward Tiffany. They chatted briefly before Priscilla made her way back to Tim. As she approached, she noticed a tall man standing beside him.

"Hey, babe, there you are," Tim said, his tone light. "I want you to meet my brother."

The man turned, and their eyes locked.

James.

Priscilla froze, her breath catching in her throat. **This can't be real.**

"James, this is my lady I've been telling you about. Priscilla, this is my brother, James."

The room seemed to tilt. Tiffany, noticing the exchange, rushed over just as Priscilla's knees buckled. She caught her friend before she hit the floor.

Confrontation

"Priscilla, you okay, baby?" James asked, kneeling beside her.

Tiffany held her head, whispering soothing words. Tim's voice cut through the moment, sharp and demanding. "James, you know my girlfriend?"

Tiffany intervened. "You two need to step outside. I'll take care of her."

As Tiffany called for a damp cloth and water, Tim and James moved toward the door.

"So, you come back to Florida and decide to scoop up my girl?" Tim spat; his voice laced with anger.

James raised his hands defensively. "What? How was I supposed to know you knew her? I've never seen you around, you've never sent a picture, and she's never mentioned you."

Tim's jaw tightened. "I'm busy with my business. I can't always be around. But that doesn't matter, she's still my girlfriend. Of all the women in South Florida, you had to go after her. This is just like you, James."

James's expression hardened. "We need to let her decide, bro. I'm not giving up—I really like her."

The Aftermath

Tim's words hung in the air—sharp, defiant. **"We will see about that,"** he said before rushing back inside.

Priscilla blinked, disoriented. Her head throbbed, and Tiffany's hands gently pressed a damp cloth against her forehead.

"What just happened?" Priscilla murmured, her voice barely above a whisper. "Did I actually see James and Tim together? And did Tim just say that James is his brother?"

Tiffany sighed. "Yes, girl. You saw right. And yeah—that's his brother."

Priscilla inhaled sharply, trying to steady herself. "They're outside now, talking?"

"They are," Tiffany confirmed. "Forget about them for now. Are you okay?"

Priscilla nodded slowly. "Hand me that water."

She took a sip, letting the coolness settle her nerves. "Help me into the chair, please."

Tiffany helped her ease into the seat just as Tim and James started approaching. Tiffany's eyes narrowed—she wasn't about to let them ruin this night.

"Oh no," she said firmly, stepping in front of them. "Not tonight. This is her night. You two need to talk to her **tomorrow**."

Tim and James exchanged glances before looking over at Priscilla. Her head was lowered, exhaustion evident in her posture.

Neither argued.

They turned and left.

The Morning After

Priscilla woke to the relentless buzz of her phone. **Twenty missed calls. Too many messages. Voicemails stacked up.**

Tim had called ten times.

James, five.

The rest were family and friends checking in.

Tiffany had stayed over, just in case.

"Hey, you up?" Tiffany called from the kitchen. "I made breakfast."

Priscilla groaned, rolling onto her side. "Coming."

After freshening up, she padded into the kitchen, the scent of eggs and cinnamon toast filling the air.

She sat down, staring at her plate before shaking her head. **This is too much.**

"Girl, was I dreaming, or did Tim and James show up at the grand opening?"

Tiffany folded her arms. "Nope. Not a dream. Brother, girl, they are *brothers*. What are the odds that you'd fall for both?"

Priscilla exhaled deeply. "Tim never talks about family. How was I supposed to know?"

Tiffany shrugged. "So, now what?"

"I had already made up my mind before last night that I was going to"

Her words stopped cold.

Tim.

Standing in the doorway.

The Showdown

"You weren't going to call me back?" Tim asked, his voice sharp, edged in frustration.

Priscilla's expression hardened as she placed her fork down. **Not today.**

"First of all, don't walk into my house questioning me like that," she said, her voice steady and firm. "If I haven't called you back, what makes you think you can just show up?"

Tim stared at her, jaw clenched, but she wasn't done.

"Second, since you interrupted my breakfast, do me a favor—put my key on the table and leave. I'll call you later."

His nostrils flared. "So, it's like that? Oh—so you want **him** now, huh?"

Tiffany's fork paused mid-air.

Priscilla slowly met his gaze. "Tim, get out of my house."

She leaned back in her chair, eyes cold. "The only person controlling what I do is **me**."

Tim's glare darkened, but Priscilla wasn't finished.

"Seems to me," she continued, "the *only* reason you're here now is because you feel threatened. If you hadn't found out about James, I wouldn't have even seen you. And let's not forget" She arched a brow. "All those weekend trips to the Keys. Early morning disappearances. Suspicious phone calls…"

Tim stiffened.

"I know all about **Stacey**."

Tiffany's head snapped up. **What?!**

"We've spoken a few times," Priscilla continued casually. "I was just waiting for you to finally tell the truth. But now?" She pushed her plate away. "I **don't** care."

Silence.

Tiffany glanced between them, speechless. **How was I just hearing about this?**

Tim swallowed hard. His pride was unraveling fast.

"But to answer your question," Priscilla said, voice unwavering, "Yes. I want **him**."

Tim stood still, emotions flickering across his face, guilt, disbelief. Slowly, he pulled the keys from his pocket, setting them onto the table.

His eyes flickered to Tiffany.

"I guess you knew all of this, huh?"

Tiffany's lips parted. "No."

Without another word, Tim turned and walked out

The Truth & Moving Forward

Tiffany's eyes widened in shock. "Priscilla! What in the world just happened? Who is Stacey? And what were you about to say before Tim barged in?"

Priscilla sighed, rubbing her temples. "Stacey is **Tim's wife**—the woman he failed to mention for **two years**."

Tiffany gasped. "What?!"

"She called me last week, asking about some work Tim was supposed to be doing for me," Priscilla explained. "I told her, 'What work? That's my boyfriend.' And that's when she hit me with the truth, Tim is her **husband**. They live in the Keys."

Tiffany's fork clattered onto her plate. "You're kidding."

"I wish," Priscilla muttered. "I told her she would never have a problem with me. I don't do husbands, and I *sure* don't do drama."

Tiffany sat back, shaking her head. "Wow."

They continued eating, allowing the weight of the conversation to settle. After breakfast, they decided to clear their minds with retail therapy—shopping, laughing, and pushing aside the chaos for a while.

A New Year, A New Love

That afternoon, James walked into the bookstore, his smile lighting up the space.

"Hey, Cill, how's it going, baby?"

Priscilla turned, beaming, and wrapped him in a tight embrace, pressing a kiss to his lips.

"Hey, baby," she murmured.

"You ready to go?"

"Just grabbing my purse," she said, slipping into the back office.

Locking up, she headed to the car, where James stood waiting. He opened the door for her, kissing her once she was inside.

She giggled. "You are such a romantic."

"You bring it out of me," he teased, then driving off.

Tonight was **New Year's Eve**, and instead of going out, they decided to host a small, intimate gathering with friends and family.

At the store, they grabbed drinks and snacks before heading to Priscilla's home.

A Night to Remember

By **eight o'clock**, guests arrived Tiff, glowing with happiness alongside her new man, a well-known real estate mogul. Priscilla's family, a few of James's cousins, though some still weren't thrilled about the whole **Tim situation**.

Music pulsed through the house, laughter spilling from every corner. Some guests lounged by the pool, others danced in the living room, while others gathered in the kitchen, savoring the spread of food.

"Okay, everybody! It's time!" James called out.

The crowd moved outside, excitement buzzing in the air. Fireworks exploded into the night sky, sparkling bursts of color reflecting over the water.

10...9...8...7...6...5...4...3...2...1—HAPPY NEW YEAR!!!!

The countdown ended, cheers filled the air, and James turned to Priscilla, his gaze tender.

"Cill, will you marry me?"

Her breath hitched.

He dropped to one knee, pulling out a ring, and the crowd erupted in gasps and cheers.

"When you know, you know," he said simply.

Tears welled in her eyes. "Yes! *Yes!* When you know, you know."

James slid the ring onto her finger just as Tiffany screamed, rushing forward. "I *knew* it! I *knew* it—from that **first** dance at Hard Rock!"

They both laughed, their embrace holding for what felt like an eternity.

A New Beginning

Next year, she will be **Mrs. Priscilla Jones**.

This had been a **mess**.

But somehow—against all the chaos—it had led her to exactly where she was meant to be.

Happy New Year.

Sneak Peek: The Next Chapter in Priscilla's Story

Life doesn't just reset—it evolves. After all the chaos, the heartbreak, and the lessons learned, Priscilla is stepping into a new beginning. The bookstore stands, the café hums with life, and for the first time in a long time, the future feels like hers to shape.

But even new beginnings come with unexpected turns.

Here's a first look at what's next for Priscilla—where fresh starts meet old shadows, and where the past might not be as far behind as she hoped.

Here We Go

Priscilla's new chapter at the bookstore is already off to a promising start, and now the café is coming to life, too.

Imagine the steady hum of morning preparations—boxes stacked near the back entrance, fresh deliveries rolling in. The scent of roasted coffee beans and warm pastries fills the air as baristas begin their rhythm, unboxing fresh supplies, setting up the pastry case, and making sure everything is just right before the first rush.

She watches from the register, taking it all in—the energy, the movement, the way her dream is unfolding, piece by piece. Customers trickle in, some drawn by the books, others lured by the promise of caffeine and conversation.

And in this moment, after everything, it's not just a business—it's a home, a place of stories, flavors, and second chances.

Priscilla looked up, taking in the exposed beams she had so carefully chosen. Stained with just the right depth of warmth, they stretched across the ceiling, grounding the space with a rustic elegance. They weren't just beams; they were part of the story—part of the vision she had fought to bring to life.

In the early days, when this place had been nothing more than an empty shell, she had imagined how those beams would frame the café, making it feel like home. Now, as the morning light filtered through the windows, highlighting their rich texture, she knew she had made the right choice.

Here, beneath them, books and coffee intertwined, conversations sparked, and fresh starts unfolded. The café wasn't just running—it was breathing, becoming.

The phone buzzed against the counter, the name flashing across the screen like an echo from a past she thought she had left behind. Tim.

She hesitated, then answered—saying nothing. Just listening.

His voice was steady, rehearsed, offering a forced congratulations to her and James, words wrapped in a facade too thin to be believable. He spoke as if he meant it, as if history hadn't unraveled between them.

Priscilla didn't respond. Didn't offer a thank you. Didn't give him the satisfaction of knowing whether his words carried any weight.

Silence stretched between them, thick and heavy, until finally, he sighed.

"Anyway… just wanted to say that."

She let the silence linger a little longer, then ended the call without a word.

Tiff and Yella walked in, laughter bubbling between them—until they caught the look on Priscilla's face. The shift in their energy was immediate.

They didn't have to ask.

Yella tilted her head, studying her, while Tiff folded her arms, waiting, as if giving Priscilla the space to speak… or the space to pretend she was fine.

The phone still sat on the counter, the screen dark now, but the weight of that call lingered in the air like an unwelcome presence.

Priscilla blinked, shook herself out of it, and forced a breath. "Deliveries came in for the café," she said, voice steady, changing the subject before they could pry.

But they weren't fooled.

Tiff nodded slowly, Yella exchanged a glance with her, and neither of them pushed. Not yet.

Priscilla kept the conversation light, making small talk as they handled the café deliveries, but Tiff and Yella weren't fooled. They knew her well enough to recognize when something was off.

Minutes later, they made their way over to the salon, slipping into her office, where the truth finally spilled out.

"The call was from Tim," she said simply, leaning against her desk, arms crossed like a shield.

Yella's reaction was instant. "Oh, wait a minute—he has a lot of nerve calling you now." Her voice sharpened, brows knitting together as she settled into full-on defense mode.

Tiff, on the other hand, remained quiet. Her lips pressed together, arms folded as she leaned against the doorframe, watching—assessing. She wasn't quick to speak, always the one to keep a level head before jumping to judgment.

Priscilla exhaled, shaking her head. "It was nothing. Just fake congratulations, empty words. I didn't even respond."

"Good," Yella muttered, crossing her arms like she was ready for war. "Because seriously? After everything?"

Tiff sighed but didn't speak—her silence said enough.

Priscilla let the moment settle. Tim's words didn't matter. But the way her friends reacted, how they stood with her, reminded her of one thing—she wasn't facing this alone.

Tiff sighed and shook her head. "Just block his calls, Priscilla."

But they all knew Tim wouldn't stop there. He'd find another way, another excuse, another reason to intrude. He always did.

Instead of lingering on it, Priscilla exhaled and shifted the energy. "Anyway," she said, leaning back in her chair, "what's the plan for the weekend?"

Yella perked up, her frustration quickly replaced with excitement. "James is doing a Sand and Sweat at the beach—his training business is really taking off."

Tiff nodded. "That's good for him. He's worked hard for this."

Priscilla allowed herself to relax into the conversation. The café, the bookstore, James's success—it was all proof that life was moving forward. No matter what ghosts tried to claw their way back.

Tiff and Yella exchanged a glance, the same unspoken thought passing between them.

"Sand and Sweat," Yella muttered, shaking her head. "He works us too hard."

Tiff sighed, stretching her arms like she was preparing for battle. "Yeah… but okay."

Priscilla laughed, knowing full well that by the end of the session, they'd all be questioning their life choices. But it wasn't just about the workout—it was about showing up, supporting James, and embracing the challenge.

Because if there was one thing they knew, pain meant progress.

The conversation shifted, the tension of Tim's call fading into something lighter, something full of promise.

"So, how's the wedding planning coming along?" Yella asked, leaning forward, eyes shining with curiosity.

Tiff leaned forward, tapping a pen against the edge of Priscilla's desk, already in full planning mode.

"Alright, so let's talk wedding," she said, pulling out a notebook—because of course she had one. "You and James settled on beachside, which is perfect. But we need to lock in the essentials—guest list, catering, décor."

Priscilla exhaled, amused but grateful. "I knew you were gonna do this."

Yella laughed. "Of course she was gonna do this."

Tiff smirked. "You need someone to keep this thing from turning into chaos. Now, tell me—what's the vibe? Classic elegance, laid-back boho, or something totally different?"

Priscilla hesitated. "Somewhere in between. Nothing too traditional, but not too casual either."

Tiff nodded. "Good. That means we're talking neutral tones with statement pieces. And the dress—are we thinking fitted, flowy, something dramatic?"

Priscilla shook her head. "I don't even know yet."

Yella rolled her eyes. "Girl, we need a shopping trip."

Tiff continued scribbling. "Fine, we'll figure it out. But you *will* have a dress picked out before the month's over. Non-negotiable."

The conversation spiraled into colors, music, and logistics until finally, it trailed off—leaving just enough unanswered, just enough lingering excitement.

Because one thing was clear: Priscilla's story wasn't done yet.

Tiff was deep into planning mode, rattling off details, jotting notes, keeping everything in check. Yella chimed in, hyping up the dress search, the color palette, the celebration ahead.

For the first time in a while, Priscilla allowed herself to lean into the excitement.

Then—her phone buzzed.

Not Tim.

Not a familiar name.

Just **Unknown Caller** staring up at her from the screen.

Her stomach tightened. The conversation around her kept going, voices overlapping, but the world had suddenly quieted in her head.

Unknown.

She hesitated. Just for a second.

Then the screen went dark, the call disappearing before she could even decide what to do.

She swallowed, forcing her focus back to the wedding plans, the laughter, the good things.

But in the back of her mind, that call lingered. A thread, a warning, a whisper from something not quite finished.

Want to know what happens next for Priscilla?

New beginnings bring unexpected challenges, old ghosts refuse to stay buried, and the future she's building is about to be tested.

Pick up your copy of **Here We Go** and dive into the next chapter of her journey—where every choice matters.

Thank you

To every reader who has picked up this book—thank you. Your time, your curiosity, and your willingness to step into Priscilla's world mean more than words can express.

To my friends and family, who have encouraged me through the highs and lows of writing, thank you for believing in this journey and in me.

To those who have shared kind words, supported my stories, and reminded me why I do this, your presence makes all the difference.

And to Priscilla—who continues to take on life, love, and all the unexpected twists—thank you for reminding us that new beginnings are always possible.

This book is for you. For us. For the stories that refuse to go untold.

Asmaraj

Book Club Notes

Made in the USA
Columbia, SC
04 May 2025